ly

Fly, fly little wing
Fly beyond imagining
The softest cloud the whitest dove
Upon the wind of Heaven's love
Past the planets and the stars
Leave this lonely world of ours
Escape the sorrow and the pain
And fly again

Fly, fly precious one
Your endless journey has begun
Take your gentle happiness
Far too beautiful for this
Cross over to the other shore
There is peace forevermore
But hold this mem'ry bittersweet
Until we meet

Fly, fly do not fear
Don't waste a breath don't shed a tear
Your heart is pure, your soul is free
Be on your way don't wait for me
Above the universe you'll climb
On beyond the hands of time
The moon will rise the sun will set
But I won't forget

Fly, fly little wing
Fly where only angels sing
Fly away, the time is right
Go now, find the light

Jean-Jaques Goldman & Phil Gladston

All God's Creatures Go To Heaven

ORIGINAL PAINTINGS BY N. A. NOËL

An Original Short Story By Amy Nolfo-Wheeler

Some of the original paintings in this book are also available as open edition prints.
For information on purchasing a print or for a free full color NOËL STUDIO catalog call:
1~800~444~6635

Library of Congress Catalog Card Number: 96-68622
ISBN   0-9652531-0-4

"FLY"
Jean-Jaques Goldman and Phil Gladston
© 1995 JRG Editions Musicales BP 3-92210 Montrouge (France)
CRB Music Publishing-3 Place Laval-Laval-Quebec (Canada)

"FLY" is performed by Celine Dion on her Epic Records release "Falling Into You"

Printed and Bound at WORZALLA, Stevens Point, Wisconsin
IAPHC 1997 Gallery of Superb Printing GOLD AWARD Winner

To my Uncle Bobby who shared my love for animals,
and my horse El Kadere who filled my life with devotion.

N.A Noël

To my Mother & Father for their love and belief in me,
and to Buster, my childhood dog and dear old friend; whose memory inspired this story.

A.A. Nolfo-Wheeler

In **H**eaven, children angels spend their days frolicking in ever blossoming gardens filled with brightly colored flowers. They play among sweet scented fruit trees on soft wind-swept grassy pathways.

In Heaven, children angels sometimes nap in the warmth of the sunlight and other times dance barefoot and spread their wings to enjoy the tickle of an occasional shower. There are no thunderstorms in Heaven, just gentle rains that are always followed by

ainbows.

Jacob is a little boy who lives in Heaven with lots of other children angels from all over the world. Jacob loves Heaven and he loves being an angel. In Heaven he was reunited with his Grandmother and Grandfather. Though only six years old he could remember his Grandmother's gentle touch and the fun he and his Grandfather had playing in his big backyard on Earth. In Heaven there is no pain or sorrow. Jacob does not feel sad that his parents are not with him; instead he rejoices that one day they will all be together again forever and ever.

Weeks passed and Jacob began to notice that his angel friends were caring for all kinds of different creatures. Some children had dogs while others had cats or bunnies or goats.

One shy, sweet, little angel, Micheal had a gentle, fuzzy llama named Minnie.

Jacob wanted a pet to care for too. On Earth he had a white puppy he called Gracie and a mouse by the name of Morsel. Morsel's favorite pastime was sitting in the palm of Jacob's hand while nibbling a piece of cheese. Gracie and Jacob would play in the park for hours and then come home to rest in the shade of Jacob's favorite tree.

One afternoon Jacob asked Angelica, a wise child angel, where the creatures in Heaven came from. Jacob admired Angelica's beautiful white dove. Angelica was delighted by Jacob's inquiry and decided he was ready to learn about his special purpose in Heaven.

"You see Jacob," whispered Angelica, "children have an important and wonderful purpose here. These extraordinary creatures that are being cared for by the children of Heaven all once had a life on Earth, just like you."

"You mean like my puppy Gracie on Earth?"

"Yes, Jacob, just like Gracie."

"Here we entrust the children angels with the care of these loyal animals. This is because little children and all of these loving pets have very similar souls. Children and their pets have a lot in common."

"I don't understand" said Jacob with a shrug, "I don't remember being anything like my puppy Gracie."

"Well you certainly didn't have a furry coat or a wagging tail," chuckled Angelica, "but your hearts were in the same place. Children and animals are both innocent; they need our gentle care, respect and love. Children and animals are two of God's greatest gifts to the world; their love is honest and true. Animals are a blessing Jacob, just like you."

"But why do the other children have animal companions and I do not?"

"Well, you were new here Jacob. Caring for an animal is a big responsibility; I felt you should take some time to get to know your new surroundings before your first assignment."

"Assignment? What assignment?"

"Your special purpose, Jacob ~ and the special purpose of all little children in Heaven is being trusted with the care of a pet. Some angels are assigned to ponies while others care for kittens, birds or even lambs!

We know that children can give animals loving attention until they are reunited with their human companions. At that time, you will receive a new animal to love. You are going to have many beautiful and enchanting animal friends here in Heaven Jacob!"

"Oh Angelica, I can't wait any longer for my assignment... may I have one soon?" Jacob's wings fluttered with anticipation.

"As a matter of fact, a friend arrived for you today, a heavenly friend whose name is Snowflake!" In an instant there was a burst of Stardust and suddenly a big fluffy bunny rabbit appeared in Jacob's arms. Jacob embraced his new friend with all the love his heart could give. He quickly gave Snowflake a kiss on the head. Jacob felt warm and happy; there were no words to express his joy. He turned toward the gardens, excited to share the arrival of his new friend with the other angels.

Just before Jacob flew away he turned back toward Angelica...

"Angelica?" He said softly, "this means that not just people go to Heaven?"

"Yes Jacob, it means all God's creatures go to Heaven."

"Even Gracie?" Jacob asked with a smile.

"Yes, Jacob, someday even Gracie."

he nd

In memory of our white rabbit, *Fluff 'n Stuff*.